Rosie's Ballet Slippers

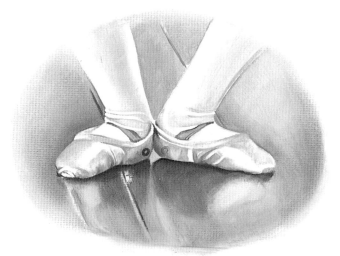

Rosie's Ballet Slippers
Text copyright © 1996 by Susan Hampshire
Illustrations copyright © 1996 by Maria Teresa Meloni
First published in Great Britain in 1996 by William Heinemann Limited, an imprint of Reed
International Books Limited.

Library of Congress Cataloging-in-Publication Data
Hampshire, Susan, date
  Rosie's ballet slippers / by Susan Hampshire ; illustrated by Maria Teresa Meloni.
   p. cm.
  Summary: During her first ballet lesson, Rosie enthusiastically learns how to point
her toes, do *pliés* and *sautés*, and dance like a butterfly.
  ISBN 0-06-026466-7. —ISBN 0-06-026504-3 (lib. bdg.)
  [1. Ballet dancing—Fiction.] I. Meloni, Maria Teresa, Ill. II. Title.
PZ7.H8176Ro 1996   95–31713
[E]—dc20   CIP
                                                             AC

1 2 3 4 5 6 7 8 9 10
❖
First American Edition, 1996

Rosie's Ballet Slippers

by Susan Hampshire
illustrated by Maria Teresa Meloni

HarperCollinsPublishers

To all children who love to dance.
S.H.

For Michael Hannagan
and to the memory of my grandfather, Dott. Ing. Luigi Meloni
M.T.M.

$\mathcal{F}$or her first ballet lesson Rosie's mother bought her a pair of pale pink ballet slippers. They were the prettiest slippers Rosie had ever seen.

Soon the day came for Rosie's first ballet lesson. The ballet teacher was called Madame.

"Hello, Rosie," she said. "Please put on your ballet slippers, and then come and meet the other children."

Rosie put on her new ballet slippers, then said hello to the other children. Their names were Tommy, Sally, Jasmine, Yuko, Rani, Chuck, and Rudolph.

"And this is Miss Melody, who plays the piano," said Madame. Miss Melody smiled at Rosie, and her fingers ran like mice up and down the piano keys.

Then it was time for the ballet lesson to begin.

"Now, children," said Madame, "sit on the floor with your legs straight out in front, and point your toes like sharp pencils."

Rosie sat in a row with the other children, and Madame showed them how to point their feet in time to the music.

"Now, what do we do after toes?" Madame asked.

"HANDS!" Rudolph shouted.

"That's right," said Madame. "I want you to shake your hands as though they're dripping with water."

Rosie shook her hands and made them as soft as rabbits' ears.

"See how pretty they look?" said Madame. "These are our ballet hands."

Then Madame gave each child one red sticker and one blue sticker. "These are to stick onto your ballet slippers. Watch me and put the red sticker on your right heel and the blue sticker on your left heel."

Rosie carefully stuck the red sticker on her right slipper and the blue sticker on her left slipper.

Then Madame showed the children how to do points.

"Girls, please hold out your skirts like butterflies. Boys, hands on hips, backs as straight as ironing boards. Now we'll do three points with the right *red* foot, then we'll change feet and do three points with the left *blue* foot."

Rosie looked down at the foot she was pointing. She could see a blue sticker, so she knew that she hadn't made a mistake.

Next they practiced skipping.

"Knees high, skirts held out, backs straight," Madame called as they skipped around the room.

Jasmine and Rani skipped so fast that they bumped into each other and fell in a heap on the floor.

When Rosie had finished skipping, she was out of breath. She was glad to stand still and do knee bends.

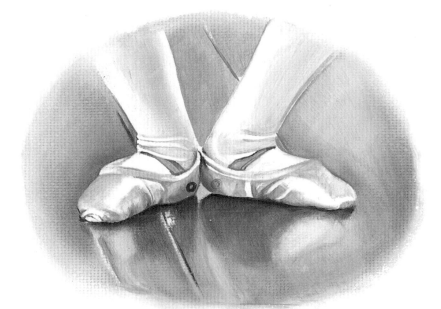

"These are *pliés* in the first position, when your heels are together," said Madame. "But when your feet are apart

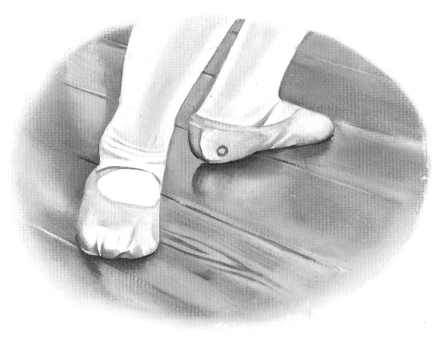

and your toes are turned out, they are *pliés* in the second position."

Then Madame showed
the children how to bend
their legs with their knees
going over their toes.

Rosie carefully put her heels together and pulled her knees straight. "I can do first position," she told Madame. "And I can do second position, too!"

"Very good, Rosie," Madame answered.

"Now, Jasmine, please show us the first, second, and fifth positions of the arms."

Jasmine started by putting her arms down below her tummy.

"This is first position," she said, with her arms out in front of her as though she was holding a basket.

Then Jasmine put her
arms out to the side like a
scarecrow.

"This is second
position," she said.

And finally she lifted them
above her head like a frame around
her face.

"Fifth position! I like fifth position
best because I feel like a real
ballerina," Jasmine said happily.

"Very nice, Jasmine," said
Madame.

"Now, who wants to jump and see if they can touch my hand with their head?" Madame asked.

"Oh, I do!" cried Tommy and Sally at the same time.

"A jump is called a *sauté*," said Madame. "Let's *sauté* with pointed toes and straight knees and see how high we can go."

"I can jump very high," said Rosie.

When the children had finished jumping, Miss Melody played some beautiful music on the piano.

"Listen to the piano," said Madame. "First we're going to dance like butterflies, and when the music changes, we're going to dance like animals."

Miss Melody played some quiet, pretty music, and Rosie ran lightly around the room fluttering her arms. Suddenly, Miss Melody started playing some loud, thumping music. Chuck and Rudolph pretended to climb trees and chased the girls.

Madame clapped her hands. "What do ballet dancers do when they have finished dancing?" she asked.

"Bow! Curtsey!" the children cried together.

"Yes, this is our *révérence*," answered Madame. "Girls, hold out your skirts, then put your right foot behind your left foot and bend your knees. Boys, put your hand across your waist, bend forward from the hips, and bow."

Rosie curtsied with the other girls. The boys bowed.

"Thank you, everyone," Madame said. "That's the end of our lesson for today. Make sure you practice at home, and I'll see you all next week."

"Did you like your ballet lesson?" asked Rosie's mother, giving her the ballet slippers to carry.

Rosie nodded and smiled as she waved good-bye to Sally. She swung the slippers by their elastic straps. She wanted everyone to see them.

But when they got back home, Rosie found that she'd lost one of her slippers.

"Oh, dear," said her mother. "We'll have to go all the way back."

Just then, there was a scratch at the door. It was Buster, Rosie's dog, with the missing ballet slipper in his mouth!

"Good dog!" Rosie exclaimed, patting him happily.

After supper, Rosie put on her ballet slippers, and practiced the steps she had learned that day.

She skipped around and around the room, pointing her toes, as Buster sat and watched her.

"I love dancing. I want to dance and dance all day."